To Kyra — our own courageous daughter.
— *K.R.*

For everyone at Ardmore Elementary, where I first learned to read.
— *M.T.*

The paintings for this book were created in watercolour and pencil
on Arches Paper.

This book was designed in QuarkXPress, with type set in 18 point Bembo.

Canadian Cataloguing in Publication Data

Trottier, Maxine
Laura : a childhood tale of Laura Secord

ISBN 0-439-98724-5

1. Secord, Laura, 1775-1868 — Juvenile fiction. I. Reczuch, Karen. II. Title.

PS8589.R685L38 2000   jC813.'54   C00-930797-4
PZ7.T7532La 2000

5 4 3 2 1   Printed and bound in Canada   0 1 2 3 4 /0

One afternoon long ago, the sun hung over a farm. It touched the corn in the fields with its heat and sparkled on the pond. The girl who walked barefoot towards the meadow felt its sweet warmth on her neck. A book in her apron pocket slapped against her leg. Each day it was the same.

"Hello, Peg," Laura always called, looking across the field for the old milk cow. As often as not, Peg would be curled there in the shade, calmly chewing her cud. Now and again Peg wandered, but Laura knew where to look for her.

"The chores are finished and it is time for a story," Laura would say. "What should I read today?"

Laura shared the chores with her sisters, but she alone took care
of Peg. Settled in the grass, her back against the cow's huge belly,
she was happy. Old Peg's calf would be born in a few days and
Laura could barely wait.

Her father shook his head, but Laura's mother only smiled.
"She loves that cow very much," she said. "You must hold tightly
to the things you love, you know."

The cow was as special to Laura as the farm was to them all. Their neighbours were good, honest folk, and the Mohican people who came to the house now and again were open and friendly.

That afternoon Laura heard a cicada begin its hot buzzing as she looked around for Peg. She shielded her eyes with her hands. The cow was not under the apple tree where she usually rested at this hour.

She was not standing in the shallow stream drinking cool
water, either. The meadow lay empty and suddenly silent.
Where was Peg? What would Mama and Papa say?

Laura felt a chill, although the sun beat down on her head.
She hurried across the meadow and entered the forest.

"Peg! Where are you, Peg?" Laura called frantically, but no welcoming moo answered.

Deeper and deeper into the woods she walked. There were bears here, she knew. Every shadow seemed to have teeth and dangerous eyes. At each snap of a twig she feared that something hungry would leap out at her.

Laura fought back the fear that weakened her legs, but she did not stop. Peg needed her.

Brambles and low branches caught at her clothing. Her braids loosened and her long hair became tangled. She swatted at insects as she called again and again for the cow.

At last the trees began to thin. The sun had dropped low in the sky and the first robins were singing their evening song. When darkness came she would be lost. Her hands were cold and sweaty at the thought of the shadowy forest and what might be in it. Would wolves be out prowling when the sun went down?

Still, Laura went on. The ground became wet and soft. Cattails and marsh marigolds appeared. Mud caked her legs and weighed down the tattered hem of her skirt.

When the moon rose and stars appeared, she stopped for a moment.
Her pounding heart and ragged breathing drowned out all other sounds.
There ahead on a grassy rise was a shape. Laura ran towards it,
then dropped down next to Peg, who lay motionless in the moonlight.

"What were you thinking, to wander off like this?" scolded Laura.
"Get up. We must find our way home." But the cow did not move. Its
eyes were closed and no warm breath came from its nostrils.

"Oh no, Peg!" cried Laura. She leaned her forehead down upon the old cow's side and wept softly. Then, above her tears and the sad music of frogs and crickets, she heard a small sound.

Laura looked up. In the shadows stood a little calf.
Its legs wobbled and its damp hair stuck to its skin.
It took a shaky step towards her.

"Poor thing," said Laura tenderly. "Do not be afraid. I will take care of you for your mother."

She stroked Peg's head gently and leaned down to whisper something into her old cow's velvety ear. Then she struggled to her feet and went to the calf. It felt warm and alive when she wrapped her arms around it.

"Let us go home," she said and she started out, looking straight ahead.
She dared not look back. It was so far and she was not certain of the
path. How would she find her way in the dark?

Laura walked slowly back across the marshy ground. The calf followed her, its legs wobbly at first, then gaining strength with each step it took. They stopped many times to rest in the darkness, the calf pressing close to Laura.

Finally, the mud of the swamp gave way to harder earth, and the dark presence of the forest rose ahead. Soon trees surrounded her. Laura heard the call of an owl.

"Hush," she whispered as the calf trembled at the sound. "I will let nothing hurt you."

Her voice sounded brave in her own ears, but the forest's night sounds, the rustling and creaking, and the distant howl of a wolf made her shiver. She stopped.

Up ahead, light wavered upon the huge tree trunks.

"Laura!" shouted her father's voice, "Where are you?"

"I am here, Papa!" called Laura as she sank down on the ground, her arms around the calf's neck. Her eyes filled with happy tears of relief.

The torchlight grew brighter as her father and a dozen Mohican men ran towards her. "What were you thinking, to wander off into the forest?" he cried. But when he saw the calf, Laura's father knew.

"Come child, let us go home," he said gently. "Let me lead the calf."

"No, I can do it," answered Laura as she rose to her feet. She looked back into the darkness where she knew Peg lay. For a moment a soft, sad wave of memory washed over her. Then she felt the calf, warm and alive at her side.

Suddenly Laura was not tired at all. "You must hold tightly to the things you love, Papa."

And her father smiled. They walked slowly together through the forest and home again, with the Mohicans leading the way.

When the farm appeared, the men waved and then drifted
into the night. In the yard Laura's mother, her face streaked
with tears, held her tired daughter close.

"You will need warm milk and a rag for this wee calf tonight,"
she said.

Papa put the calf in the barn while Mama warmed milk.

Laura washed the mud from her arms and legs. Then, in her shift, surrounded by the sweet smell of hay in the barn, she fed the calf. At last, sleepy and full of milk, it lay its head upon her lap and slept.

Laura's father watched her. She was a strong girl with a brave and loving heart. She would be a stronger woman, he thought proudly.

"Peg," Laura whispered. "I will call you Peg."

She pulled out a book. And, as the pigeons in the loft cooed softly and the moon set in the night beyond the barn's still walls, Laura began to read.

*L*aura Ingersoll was born in Massachusetts in 1775. Her father, Thomas Ingersoll, was an officer in the Colonial Militia during the Revolutionary War. Laura's childhood and that of her sisters would have been deeply coloured by the war, in the way such things always affect children. Yet it seems that she emerged strong and whole. In 1795 the Ingersolls moved to Upper Canada, and in 1797 Laura married James Secord. In 1803 they built a home in the village of Queenston; that house still stands.

Some years later, during the War of 1812, Queenston was captured by the Americans. Somehow Laura learned that the American forces were planning a surprise attack on the British troops at Beaver Dams. One story suggests that the enemy officers forced their way into the Secord home demanding food. As they ate, Laura overheard their plans. She knew that unless the British officer, Lieutenant FitzGibbon, was warned, the Niagara Peninsula would be lost.

The next day Laura set off at dawn to warn the British. Some versions of her story say that she led her milk cow as a diversion, but this is unlikely. She walked all day in the June heat and that night crossed the Black Swamp. As she struggled up the Niagara escarpment, she was stopped by a band of Iroquois. One of them led her to Lieutenant FitzGibbon. She had walked thirty kilometres, and when the Americans attacked, the British were ready.

This story is a work of fiction, but at its heart there is a core of truth. Laura Secord was a brave woman and a Canadian hero. Like many people who have come to this country, she had the courage to survive and build her life on the strength of what she believed and what she loved.